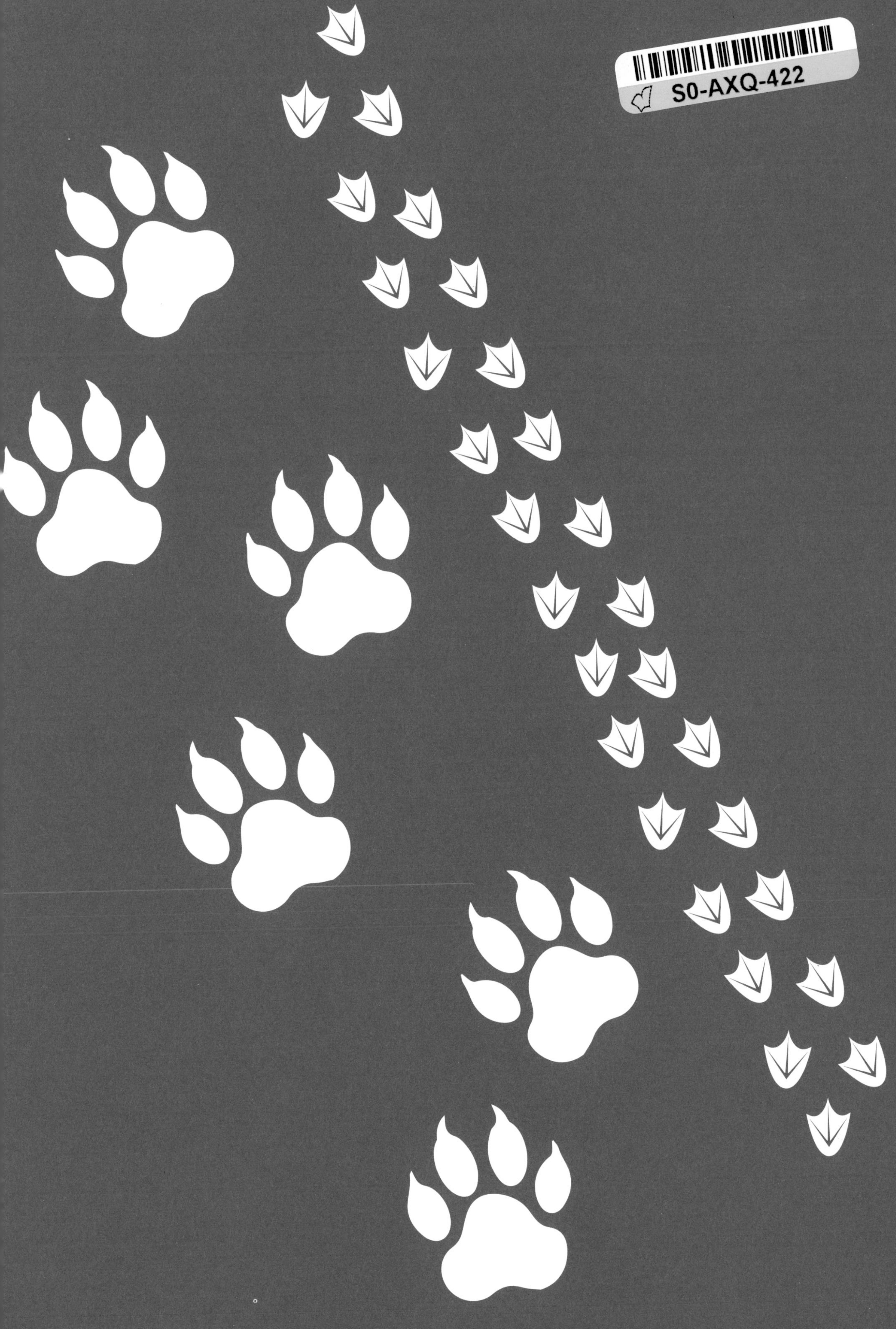

A Surprising Friendship

written by Andrew Wald   illustrations by Tara J. Hannon

DEEPER
WELL
PUBLISHING

Dedication

Thank you to my dear wife Tess
for her love, enduring support, and
editorial assistance. Thank you also to my
son Ben, his wife Alicia, and my daughter
Leah and her husband Jacob, for their
continual belief in this book.

Thank You

I want to thank Tara J. Hannon for creating
the beautiful illustrations I had envisioned to
make the story come alive. I also want the
thank my publisher, Anthony J.W. Benson,
for his expert guidance and advice from
beginning to end.

ISBN: 978-0-9857152-8-1

Library of Congress Control Number: 2019917738

DEEPER
WELL
PUBLISHING

Published 2020 Printed in the United States

Written by Andrew Wald
Illustrated by Tara J. Hannon
Creative Director: Anthony J.W. Benson, injoiCreative.com
Design by CharLee Christian and Anthony J.W. Benson

Way up in northern Canada, far from
any people, there was a beautiful pond. Zoey,
a playful Canadian goose, loved swimming
on the pond.

4

The cool water felt
refreshing in the hot July sun.

One day, Zoey heard a rustling in a blackberry bush nearby.

Suddenly, a striking bear appeared. Startled, Zoey gasped,
"Yikes! I didn't know there were bears around here. Who are you?"

The bear quickly explained, "Oh, I'm sorry if I surprised you.
My name is Henry." In a friendly voice, Henry continued,
"I just moved here from the other side of the river.
By the way, what's your name?"

"I'm Zoey. This is my pond.
Well, it's not really mine. I call it my pond
because I love it and I spend so much time
here." Zoey paused, and then asked in a
somewhat fearful voice...

7

"No, no, don't worry," laughed Henry. "I mostly eat berries, and I really love fish."

Feeling greatly relieved, Zoey exclaimed, "I like fish too! Would you like to come in for a swim? The water feels great and there are tons of fish in here."

"That sounds great!" Henry said excitedly. Henry jumped in the water making a huge splash. The ripples reached all the way to the other side of the pond. When Henry shook the water away from his face and looked around, he smiled and told Zoey, "I can see why you spend so much time here. This place is awesome!"

Zoey and Henry spent the rest of the day swimming and playing together.

From that day forward, they would meet
at the pond every day, laughing and playing from
sunrise to sunset. As the days passed,
their friendship grew stronger and stronger.

Sometimes, they would have
water contests, like seeing who could
hold their breath under water the
longest. Zoey usually won.

Or, they would see who could catch the biggest
fish. Henry's fish was usually much larger.

Neither of them really
cared about winning.

They just loved playing
together, day after day.

Many weeks passed, and summer began to leave.

Fall arrived bringing many changes.

One morning, they noticed the pond was partially frozen at the water's edge. They also noticed that the sun was setting earlier, cutting short their playtime.

There were other changes too. Lately, while they were playing, Henry would yawn a great big yawn. Zoey had never seen Henry yawn like that before. So, she asked Henry, "Are you all right?"

"Oh, I'm okay. Just feeling a little tired," Henry replied with another long yawn.

Also, Henry noticed Zoey often looking up at the sky.
So, he asked her, "What are you looking at Zoey?"

"I just see my friends flying south and feel I should
join them. But don't worry, I would rather be here with you,"
Zoey reassured Henry.

As Fall settled in, the weather felt colder and colder. Zoey watched Henry moving slower and yawning more. Although Henry was feeling very tired and needed to sleep through the winter, he didn't want to stop playing.

Also, Henry noticed Zoey gazing longer and longer at her flying friends. Zoey tried hard to ignore her growing desire to fly south with her friends.

Finally, one snowy morning, Henry sadly confessed,
"I'm so sorry Zoey, but I'm too tired to play. I want to, but
I just can't. I really need to sleep."

Zoey reassured Henry, "That's all right,"
she said shivering. "I'm feeling too cold to play anyway.
I love playing with you, but I have to go where it's warmer."

Both felt sad because they knew they had to be
apart. Henry sighed, "Zoey, you're my best friend
and I'm really going to miss you."

22

"You're mine too," Zoey said. Then, looking straight at Henry, she whispered, "And I'm going to miss you more."

So, they made a promise to meet at the pond
when the weather turned warm again. As they parted,
they both thought about their deep friendship.

As Henry crawled into his winter bed,
he smiled a big bear smile.

He decided he would dream all winter
about playing with Zoey on their pond.

After several months, the snow melted, and Henry began to wake up. He yawned and stretched as he gazed at the green grass and colorful spring flowers all around him.

Suddenly, he remembered the pond. He thought to himself, "Was it a dream or was it real?" He had to find out. So, he lumbered over to the pond.

The first thing he saw, laying next to the pond, was a small stack of berries.

Then he heard a familiar voice coming from the middle of the pond.

"They're for you," the voice said cheerfully.

Henry smiled.

30

The End

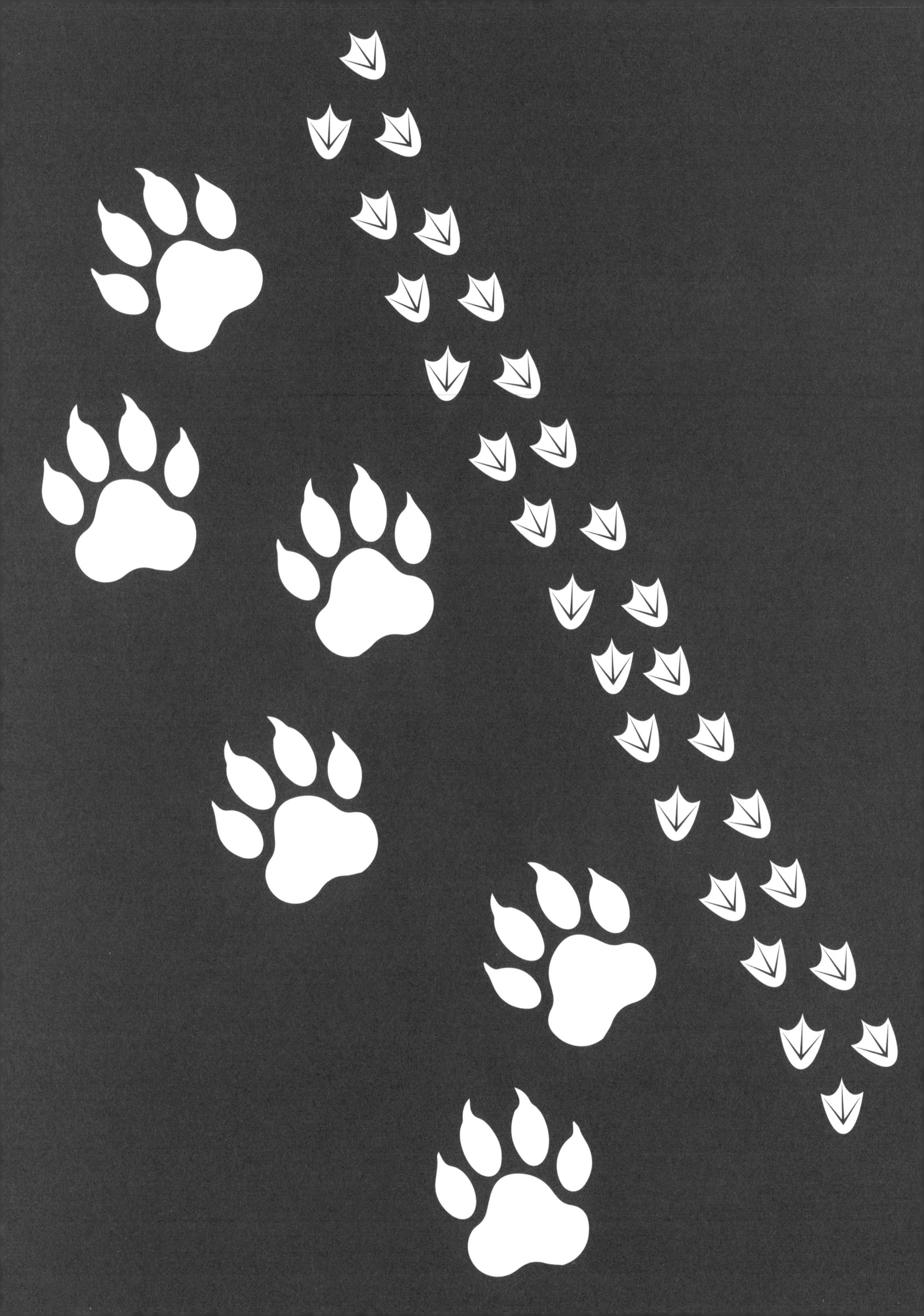